O. W Gates, publisher "World" Book and Job Printing House

Glimpses of San Diego, Historic and Prophetic

A Poem

O. W Gates, publisher "World" Book and Job Printing House

Glimpses of San Diego, Historic and Prophetic
A Poem

ISBN/EAN: 9783744711821

Printed in Europe, USA, Canada, Australia, Japan

Cover: Foto ©Andreas Hilbeck / pixelio.de

More available books at **www.hansebooks.com**

GLIMPSES OF SAN DIEGO,

HISTORIC AND PROPHETIC,

A POEM.

READ BY

REV. O. W. GATES,

BEFORE

THE CLIOTHEAN SOCIETY

—OF—

POINT LOMA SEMINARY,

San Diego, Cal., August 12th, 1875.

SAN DIEGO:
"WORLD" BOOK AND JOB PRINTING HOUSE.
1875.

CORRESPONDENCE.

Rev. O. W. Gates—
Dear Sir: The young ladies of the "Cliothean Society" request for publication a copy of your Poem— "Glimpses of San Diego, Historic and Prophetic," delivered before the Society in Horton's Hall on the Second Anniver- sary of Point Loma Seminary, August 12th, 1875;

> Verna Overbaugh, ⎫
> G. Shellenberger, ⎬ Committee.
> Lina Schumacher, ⎭

San Diego, Cal., August 20, 1875.

Misses Overbaugh, Shellenberger and Schumacher:— In reply to your note requesting for publication a copy of the Poem read before your Society at the Anniversary of Point Loma Seminary, permit me to say, it was written without any thought of its coming before the public in printed form; but being assured that your request expresses the wish of many others, I will comply.

Very respectfully,
O. W. Gates.

San Diego, Cal., August 25, 1875.

[II]

INTRODUCTION.

The Poem, friends, that you expect to hear,
May well, I think, be called *the child of fear!*
When asked to write in verse, I **was** *afraid*
My truant muse beyond recall had strayed;
No sooner subject had I sought and chose,
Than *fear* advised, "you'd better write in prose."
I pushed ahead, but *fear* assailed my mind—
" Good poetry is very hard to find."
I made some progress—doubtless like a snail—
" Too slow," cried *fear*, "in *quantity* you'll fail;"
Work told; it always tells, when good, and true,
But *fear* reproached, " you never will get through;"
I did, nathless, look! doubt it if you will;
Then *fear* affirmed "you've made too big a pill;"
I *fear* I have, but still must frankly own,
Just how to split the pill I have not known;
Upon whichever part my choice may hit,
You'll wish, I *fear*, that *that* were marked "omit."—
Enough of this; another thread I'll spin,
Lest *fear* plague *you* that I cannot begin.

GLIMPSES OF SAN DIEGO.

DEVELOPMENT IN CREATION AND HISTORY GRADUAL.

Who patient scans with scrutinizing gaze
The rock-kept records of primeval days,
Will find this key unlocks the covert plan:
By each creative act the Lord foreshadowed man.
So he who reads the lesser, outspread page
Where Clio writes, as age succeeds to age,
Of busy brains concocting schemes untold,
Of roving feet in search of hidden gold,
Of direful War and all the woe he brings,
Of smiling Peace and all the songs she sings,
Of nations wrapped in all the pomp of power,
Or cast to earth to rise again no more,
Of kingdoms rent and empires on the wane,
Their glory gone and gone their right to reign,
Of hostile claims maintained by clash of swords,
Or noble aims advanced by worthy words,
Can, in the net-work of commingling lines,
Find traces plain and undeceiving signs,
That grand events, infolding good sublime
Are seen in outline long before their time,
But wait, like buds, concealing embryo blooms,
Till Winter dies, and Spring, reviving, comes.

Glimpses of San Diego.

CALIFORNIA AN EXAMPLE.

Hail California! —Name of magic spell,
What tongue first spoke thee, tongue shall never tell.
What language claims thee, gave thee to the race,
No skill linguistic has the power to trace.
Thy hand may reach to earliest days of yore,
And lay its grasp on hoary Aryan lore.
Thy germ may come from old Hebraic shoots,
Or draw its life from Greek or Roman roots,
May hold in trust some Aztec form or rite,
Or tell some tale of Mexican delight;
But ah! the secret thou hast kept thine own,
Locked in thy heart—and never to be known.
We murmur not, nor care whence rose thy name,
'Twill shine undimmed upon the scroll of fame,
Its lustre brightening as the years go by,
Like ruddy East when morning paints the sky.
So hail, once more, queen regnant of the West;
A world attentive waits for thy behest,
Looks where thy fields are piled with sacks for sheaves,
Where drop thy fruits as drop the Autumn leaves;
Turns where thy sons thy golden veins explore,
And draw in streams thy wealth of long-kept ore,
Then walks thy plains where countless flowers arise,
And gem thy face as stars thy peerless skies.
Alone, unmatched, just like thy giant trees,
Thy fame shall fly on wings of every breeze,
Sail with the ships that plow the ocean plain,
Fly on the track of each outgoing train,

Glimpses of San Diego.

Speak in thy treasures as they find their way,
In streams increasing every passing day,
Leap with each spark that thrills electric wires
To light afresh hope's half-extinguished fires.

TRIBUTE TO CALIFORNIA.

But why sing on? or why this strain prolong?
A theme so vast demands a nobler song.
Like her long-lived, decay-resisting palms,
The land of David lives in David's psalms.
Greece lives in Homer; Virgil rose and spoke
For martial Rome; then Dante came and woke
For his loved Italy, sad, deathless strains,
As Ossian sang his Scandinavian plains,
Or bard of Avon photographed his age,
And latest time will read the pictured page.
Thou too, broad land, some time shalt find a tongue
To tell the world what *Harte* has left unsung.
So, mother State, accept our filial vow,
And bind this garland on thy shining brow.
Long may thy borders rest in perfect peace;
As years roll on, may worth and wealth increase,
May faithful sons through all thy length be found;
May love-lit homes on every hand abound;
May learning rear for thee her shielding walls,
And art, with science, deck thy classic halls;
May truth divine, spread wide and far her light,
And holy faith keep all thy altars bright,

Nor chance appear for error, wrong, or crime,
To loose thy grasp on destiny sublime.
Thus live, O State, secure from every ill,
So large an orb our Muse despairs to fill,
But, venturing less, for skiffs keep near the shore,
Will trace the men and fading scenes of yore,
And mark the steps of joy and now of woe,
Whence sprang this town a century ago.
Then, should our Muse gain courage as she sings,
Her eye grow clear, and strong her unused wings,
She may attempt, led on by faith's strong hand,
To tell in verse your later "promised land."

SAN DIEGO.

Hail, San Diego! first of all the names,
That hold in trust a mission's ancient claims.
'Neath thine, no doubt, some mystic volume lies,
Its pages hid from all inquiring eyes,
Securely clasped its lid no hand may lift,
Bequeathed to time, time guards her sacred gift,
A secret safe, since question her who may,
She answers not; nor motions "yea," or "nay."

JESUITS.

Not thus concealed is every track and trace
Of those stern men who hied from place to place,
To danger deaf, not counting earthly loss,
Their zeal aflame to bear and plant the cross;

Glimpses of San Diego.

Bound by their oath to bravely do and dare,
They marched abroad for labor anywhere.
Ease, pleasure, comfort, all they freely gave
To live and serve, or fill an early grave.
Fanatics were they, well, no doubt 'tis true,
But e'en from Jesuits hold not honor due.
Go where you will through earth's extended zones,
You find the mounds where rest their wasting bones;
Look where you will some footprint will appear
Of Jesuit monk fulfilling his career.

LOYOLA.

Be patient, friends, chide not these long delays,
On men and scenes of past and buried days;
The Jesuit name calls up the daring man,
Founder at once and leader of the clan,
The monk Loyola, friend in youth of kings,
Hence spared the ills that want to many brings,
A chevalier, devoted to the dance,
Wild sport his joy, with bow, and sword, and lance,
Ambitious too, for place among the names,
That fame repeats and gratitude proclaims
Her sacred trust, her treasure, and her pride,
While time endures and rolling centuries glide.
Loyola fought in threatened citadel,
As heroes fight, and, fighting, wounded fell.
For many days hung even poised the strife
'Twixt frowning death and half extinguished life;

Glimpses of San Diego.

Life held the field; his rallied forces hurled
The grim assailant to his own dark world.
How changed the man! how changed his aims and cares!
From carnal joys, he turns to fasts and prayers,
From wealth and pomp, and royal courts and halls,
He flies to hermit cell in cloistered walls,
And there, in gloom as deep as starless night,
His vow is made and he enrolled a knight.
All that he has of genius, influence, fame,
All that he hopes by sacrifice to gain,
To Virgin, Pope, and Romish Church are given;
Their favor won, he asks no other heaven.
Let them but speak, his hand the sword shall draw,
Their uttered word shall be his "higher law."
The work assigned no scruples shall oppose;
He merits most, who most intolerance shows.
Misguided man! O had'st thou found the streams
Of living truth, in place of mocking dreams,
O had'st thou learned of Christ to seek and save,
What fadeless light had shone above thy grave;
What garlands fresh, of memory's choicest flowers,
Had kept thy name embalmed for us and ours!

LOYOLA'S SONS AS FOOTBALLS.

In sport at football, 'tis the aim of all
To hit and drive the unresisting ball.
In kindred games by men and nations played,
Loyola's sons have oft been footballs made,

Glimpses of San Diego.

Tossed hither, thither, never let alone,
In favor now, now exiled and unknown.
E'en father Pope, and holy mother Church,
Though rather slow and often in the lurch,
Have had a fancy for this stirring game,
And kept it up till somewhat bruised and lame.

FRANCISCANS IN LOWER CALIFORNIA.

In such a game played on the lower coast,
This Jesuit ball across the line was tossed
By sons of Rome, who, masters to command,
By right of might, enjoyed the conquered land.
Charles Third, of Spain,—of course he could not err,—
By royal word made haste to grant transfer
Of missions, buildings, flocks and herds, and land,
To favored fathers of Saint Francis' band,
Who, holding fast their rich and ill got store,
Unsatisfied, were reaching out for more.
Hence, as they wrought, their thought to Northward flew
To broader fields, to scenes both strange and new.
Nor can they rest; they hear a sovereign word,
"Go plant the cross where Christ was never heard."
Like soldiers true, they ask for no delay;
At order given, they rise and march away,
Some to the ships to lade the needful store,
While some, in bands will march along the shore.

Glimpses of San Diego.

Scarce loosed from bonds, o'er paths no eye can see,
Their loaded ships, strong camels of the sea,
Track watery wastes, more treacherous than the sands,
That hold entombed the wealth of Bedouin bands.
Not long had breezes filled their hoisted sails,
When ocean's wrath 'woke furious storms and gales,
Which, at command, their onward course oppose,
As army waves resist invading foes.
Disease and death, wolves lurking everywhere,
Hung on their track, with angry howl and glare,
As days went by and nights on slow wings flew,
And, in their greed, full many a victim slew.
Want too, a fiend, as cruel as the grave,
Fought full of rage these voyagers on the wave.
What wonder then that most were snatched away,
And stiff, and still, in ocean's bosom lay?
And when on land, the muster roll was read,
Silence replied, "enrolled among the dead?"
What of the march from Villacata led,
With father Crespo as its sacred head?
The ills endured, the trials on the way,
Were transient things, departing with each day.
One fact remains; no change shall it efface;
Your city's name, named then their resting place.
A choice well made. Ah, name that cannot die!
Take, San Diego, take thy destiny!

Glimpses of San Diego.

Claim thou thy right, can aught thy right debar?
Bide thou thy time, can it be distant far?
Demand thy throne, made thine by sure bequest,
And reign a queen unrivalled East and West!

FATHERS PICTURED.

Those mission fathers! Ah! I see them now,
Castilian firmness lined on every brow,
Of stately mien, whereon was plainest trace
Of strength Iberian, blent with Moorish grace,
Robust of frame, strong, hardy, full of zeal,
Courageous, cool, with curbed and conquered will,
Endurance speaking in each steady eye;
The nerve is theirs all danger to defy;
Their faces glow with fires of kindly thought,
Their souls aspire to deeds unselfish wrought,
Their lives are simple, conscientious, true,
Their virtues shine with such a pleasing hue,
As hides in part, but gives no just excuse,
For errors held, and power's prolonged abuse.
Without attaining life's sublimest plan,
They yet did good and served their brother man.
Well, earnest men, our song ungrudging pays,
Your clouded worth its proper meed of praise.
The breadth and scope of love-awakened powers
Were then unknown. Your age was not as ours.

Glimpses of San Diego.

QUERY.

What if those men of English pilgrim stock,
Who first set foot on ice bound Plymouth rock,
And faced serene, such crushing Winter woes,
As want, and frost, disease and driving snows,
Who wrung their food from hard and rocky soil,
By sweat of face and never resting toil,
And knew no good that was not dearly bought,
Nor held a prize for which they had not fought,
Had passed Point Loma, that December day,
And moored the Mayflower in this peaceful bay,
The shore and sea in sunshine all aglow,
While yon tall heads wore only locks of snow,
And then, from hence, had found their way abroad,
To plant their schools and give the living word?
Ah, well—*what if?*—It is not wrong to guess,
This chosen race, led through the wilderness,
And thus made pure by their Refiner's hand,
Received in trust this Canaan as their land,
Prepared to give whatever spot they trod,
To equal rights, Soul liberty, and God.

MAY.

May, mild, sweet May, o'er all the fields is queen;
The flowers, her maids, wear robes of gold and green;
Young life keeps watch beside her ancient throne,
And pays thereat its sovereignty alone.

Glimpses of San Diego.

Her herald, beauty, waits her word to fly
A glad evangel to the earth and sky.
Her ministers of state are tall and bearded trees,
Unbent by age, majestic, yet at ease;
Her choral bands of music and of song
Wake sweetest notes and then those notes prolong,
While far abroad, her martial host appears
On dress parade, the sage, with lifted spears.
May, thus enthroned, with ease and queenly grace,
Spoke welcome words and gave the fathers place.
"Go seek the spot by nature made most fair,
Plant there your cross, rear up your altars there,
My sister queens, of equal rank and power,
Will each approve, and each her blessings shower."
Long live these queens! Their gifts unstinted fall,
By Wealth's abode, and Poverty's thatched wall.
Since first the fathers in Saint Francis' name,
O'er yon fair vale, spread out their patron's claim,
Each queen, in turn, one hundred times and more,
Has held her court and ruled this sunny shore.

AT THE MISSION.

Ah! here we stand by mission walls first piled,
And scan the scenes that on their builders smiled.
Say, O ye plains, that now before me lie,
Were ye more fair to their enraptured eye?
And ye glad hills, must ye in truth confess,
Your robes have lost some charm of loveliness?

Glimpses of San Diego.

O monarch mountains, say, if e'er than now,
Did richer gems adorn your sun-lit brow?
How could the crown my wondering eyes behold,
To others seem more like illumined gold?
Ye skies above, we lift our voice to you,
Has one shade faded from your arch of blue?
Or Time's rough touch been able once to mar,
The diamond glisten of a single star?
O ye bright clouds of chalcedony mist,
And you, ye argosies, of amethyst,
And ye, of amber, with your sails all set,
Borne slow along through isles of violet,
Did banners brighter ever greet the breeze,
Than now ye wave above the ether seas?
And thou, old Ocean, last to thee we seek,
Say, hast thou changed? lift up thy voice and speak!
But why the need?   A soul that loved thee well,
Had genius' tongue and could thy secrets tell,
Has sung thy song, unequaled, unsurpassed,
In strains sublime, that must all change out-last,
"Time writes no wrinkle on thine azure brow,
As at creation's dawn thou rollest now."

EARLY SCENES.

Turn, truant Thought, awhile to pensive ways;
Turn roving eye, and on these ruins gaze.
A pall of sadness hangs on every part,
A voice of grief appeals to every heart,

Glimpses of San Diego.

For ruins speak;—in tones inspired of woe,
Of wasted lives, of hopes and homes laid low,
Of buried thrones, of kings and kingdoms crushed,
Of cities waste, their mirth and music hushed,
Of sacred fanes, deserted, plundered, rent,
And all they held to dark oblivion sent.
Beside these walls that harsh decay has marred,
Within these rooms all seamed and rudely scarred,
Along these paths whose course we scarce can trace,
Beneath these palms of solitary grace,
In olive groves, where kindly nature weaves
Her curious web of yearly fruit and leaves,
Here at the pool, all broken, torn and dried,
How like the men whose graves are at its side!
Where'er we turn by meditation led,
The past comes back, and with it those long dead.
I see them now:—Thought's eye, time never dims;
I hear their songs, their sacred chants and hymns,
I stand among them joined in friendly clans,
Note their debates and how they form their plans,
I heed the father chosen to command,
Assign the service suited to each hand,
Make known his will—the law that each obeys,
With ready zeal, nor murmers nor delays.
See, on the plain, some shape adobe bricks,
Or stack them dried, like gathered grain, in ricks,
Or set on guard, are eyes for those who toil,
Or, axe in hand, go forth for woody spoil.

Glimpses of San Diego.

Some till the land for sowing precious grain,
And wait in hope the softening Winter rain,
Some give their thoughts to more domestic cares,
Or serve in turn, in penance, fasts and prayers.
These watch the flocks—so did the men of old—
And those seek sheep for Christ the shepherd's fold,
Lost sheep, whom wolves have scattered far and wide,
But sheep indeed for whom the Savior died.
Oh men! make haste, and call with winning voice,
One sheep brought back shall make all heaven rejoice.
Thus days and weeks on hasty wings flew by,
Till Winter's signs were spread athwart the sky,
Till rains came down, and earth, long parched, was cheered,
And life renewed, on hill and plain appeared.
Ah, spots are few where even lovely May
Breathes softer airs than this December day.

SABBATH SERVICE.

'Tis Sabbath now; in service all unite,
And find therein true rest and pure delight.
The hour and scene recall their early vows,
That day a convert at their altar bows,
The soul first won, attracted to their ranks,
To learn their faith and mode of giving thanks.
While nature smiles and skies serenely beam,
And Indian eyes in stoic wonder gleam,
The ruling father, self possessed and calm,
In Latin speech, reads this selected psalm:

Glimpses of San Diego.

"Except the Lord build up the house begun,
The builders' work shall quickly be undone;
Except the Lord the city safely keep,
In vain the watch resists the call of sleep;
Except the Lord calm all your rising fears,
In vain your care, your labor, grief and tears.
Learn, brothers, hence, to wait and work in trust
That God in time will lift us from the dust,
Will on our work his richest blessings shower,
And make it speak in witness of His power."
With many words like these he cheered and taught;
Truth never fails, but error comes to nought.
He scarce had ceased, when voices clear and strong,
To suited notes, poured forth this new made song,
Till echoes woke and rolled the clarion strains,
A wave of music sweeping o'er the plains.

SONG.

Keen drop the star shafts through the air,
   Bright sails the moon above,
The arching skies such brilliance wear,
   They seem a type of love.
And, mother earth, peace on thy hills,
   Inspires a holy calm;
Life, everywhere, with rapture thrills,
   And sings its oft sung psalm.
O Nature's God, in glory throned
   Far, far above our ken,

Glimpses of San Diego.

What wealth of beauty Thou hast loaned
  To aid the joy of men!

Since first we chose this hallowed spot,
  And knelt hereon for prayer.
Thy goodness, Lord, has failed us not,
  Nor failed Thy tender care.
Could hearts so blest, or hands refuse
  To rear for Thee this wall?
No, toil is bliss, if but the dews
  Of grace around it fall—
E'en as the manna, heavenly fare
  Fell in such rich supplies.
As on Want's night of black despair,
  Made Plenty's morning rise.

Thy glorious name, O Christ, we bless,
  That one lost soul is found,
The pledge, we trust, this wilderness,
  Shall yet be holy ground.
In faith Thy promises we plead;
  Give Zion large increase;
All hungry souls in mercy feed;
  All sin-bound souls release.
Long may these slowly rising towers
  Re-echo songs of praise;
The harbingers of good in showers,
  And near millennial days.

Glimpses of San Diego.

LIFE IS TWO-FOLD.

Two lives have men; one outward, one unseen,
The first is known; not so the life within.
This fact apply. When institutions start,
Two streams break forth, but ever flow apart:
This, still, and hidden, shuns the light of day,
While *that*, aloud goes talking on its way.
Unwelcome grief that Pain's fierce fire distills,
Those hidden joys that flow in quiet rills,
Contritions tear blent with the secret sigh,
Hot sweat beads wrung from souls in agony,
Blood trickling down from wounds that never heal,
Soft falling dews, the life of blighted zeal,
The pelting rain of Sorrow's cloudy hours,
When, strong, unstaid, come down the chilling showers,
These are the springs—though there are scores besides—
Of that hushed stream, which on in darkness glides
Unchecked, while years are counted slowly o'er,
To lose itself on some Lethean shore.
The other stream, e'en when its course is done,
By written word tells *how* its race was run,
Shows where it grew, made strong by confluent flood,
How shunned the spot where opposition stood;
Shows whence it took, and where its burden dropped,
How high it rose, and where its flood-tide stopped;
It wrote its life, then threw the book away,
And lo! that book is proof against decay.

Glimpses of San Diego.

Who will may read its broad and open page
Not marred by change nor blurred by growing age.
Thoughts, aims and plans wrought out in stubborn facts,
Ennobling words the seeds of mighty acts,
Broad acres tilled, so too, the acres cleared,
Buildings designed, and then by labor reared,
Vines taking root and spreading wide their hands,
Dates, figs and olives brought from other lands,
Increasing wealth of roving flocks and herds,
Triumphs achieved alike by pens and swords,
The round of toil wherein each brother strives,
The converts won and trained to broader lives,
These are the springs—though there are scores besides—
Of that *seen* stream which, talking, onward glides;
Expands, and swells, and rolls with noisy rush,
And, wanting room, gives either bank a push.
The figure take; for Clio's pen will tell
Whoever asks, or takes the time to dwell
Upon the growth the Mission tree attained,
What fruit it bore, what place and strength it gained,
Wherein it failed, how withered, and then died,
Because from Truth its root was not supplied.

KEPT FOR FREEDOM.

Oh! had the fathers with enlightened eyes
Discovered half the rich and tempting prize,
That lay concealed within this land of gold,
What altered page its history had unrolled !

Glimpses of San Diego.

Why did they not?   We wait amazed and dumb,
And hear—"Not yet, its *very time* had come."
A mind All-wise locked here exhaustless stores,
Till Freedom's flag had waved along these shores,
And Freedom's sons had 'neath its folds upreared
Homes lit by love, by woman's presence cheered,
Retreats of joy, where Virtue builds her throne
A nation's hope—a nation's corner stone.

APOLOGY.

Slow moves my song; but do not yet complain;
The old-time car was not our lightning train.
Have patience then, while our slow muse unrolls,
And paints in song the scenes of ancient scrolls;
And though her strains fall far less soft and sweet,
Upon your ears and souls that wait to greet,
Than those once waked by fingers more on fire,
From Orpheus' harp or bright Apollo's lyre,
Still follow on, and trust some glad surprise,
Lurks where she leads and waits her word, to rise
A scene of beauty that with joy shall thrill,
And give reward for care, delay, and ill.

INDIANS.

A fading race! lo, such our land contains!
A small, poor remnant, now, alas, remains!
Like picture dim, and faint in every trace,
Which wasting time will wholly soon efface;

Or, like some trunk despoiled of robe and crown,
Left all alone, its fellows smitten down
By woodman's axe, it yields to sure decay,
A sad memorial of a better day.
Ye name them SAVAGE—call them fierce and wild,
As if kind heaven had never on them smiled,
As if the blood that warms their souls and ours,
Were gift to each from strangely adverse powers—
Theirs, hot and stained by passions hell has sent,
Ours, mild and pure by heavenly charms inblent.
Ah, no, indeed! the one Almighty Lord,
Who rules all worlds, yea, made them by His word,
Knows man *as man*, and in all living souls,
Where life divine, a tide immortal rolls,
His image sees, a pledge and proof alone
That, fatherhood, the weakest child will own,
E'en when the crown of innocence is lost,
His honor gone, his glory trailed in dust,
His aims depraved, his destiny obscured,
And he a slave by sinful snares allured.
Though prodigal and outcast, man may roam,
His heaven-born soul will whisper oft of home;
Thus diamonds keep, when mud beclouds their sheen,
A heart unchanged, whose flame pulse throbs unseen.
True, brother men, your and your fathers' might
By patient toil has won the lofty height,
Whence, proud and strong, confessed a ruling race,
Ye dare disdain these men of darker face,

Glimpses of San Diego.

Whose fame ancestral in noon brightness shone
When your rude fathers were as yet unknown.
The fact is clear, and, certified, remains,
Your Saxon blood once flowed in pirates' veins;
The Angles too, so it is understood,
Were not averse to human flesh and blood.
Of all the prides, the pride of race, I ween,
When weighed aright will lightest folly seem.
You may at length hold all the Indian lands,
May see the last of almost countless bands
Of warriors brave, who felt as patriots feel,
Who fought and died—their hearts as true as steel;—
You may assert these tribes bequeath no past,
Enriched with art, aglow with names to last;
Aye, you may ask, what men they gave to please,
Like Chion Homer, or Praxiteles,
Whose songs will live, whose speaking canvass glow
Till Time's swift stream shall cease its onward flow.
An answer comes from ruins that abound
From Panama to far off Nootka's Sound,
And witness bears, to him who wisely heeds,
"These were the works of men of mighty deeds."
Oh, by your love of country, home and God,
And as ye dread Jehovah's chastening rod,
Be kindly just, so long as one remains,
Of all the men whose names are on your plains—
Names, you will use till lips shall speak no more,
Names, that are stamped on this Pacific shore,

Glimpses of San Diego.

And hence must pass like gifts from sire to son,
While mountains stand and streams to ocean run.

POSSIBLE DESTINY OF THE INDIANS.

"*It might have been!*"   Regret inspires this thought.
What might have been, before your eyes is wrought.
So turn and look like John the Patmos seer,
And grasp with him a Revelation clear.
While he beheld, the dark "*To be*" grew bright,
While you behold the wondrous "*Is*" sheds light;
What God *would do*, in vision met his eyes,
What God *has done*, to you anew shall rise.
In mid Pacific, on Hawaiian isles,
Behold the change! Lo, moral beauty smiles,
The fruit of toil for men all ripe for woe.
Sunk deep in sin—say, are there depths below?—
To them, exposed, Love sent the hand of Toil,
And nerved it well to save the precious spoil;
Unwearied, strong, sublimest deed it wrought
And won the field though Error's legions fought.
It broke the chains from marred and helpless souls,
Brought near the Christ who heals, redeems, controls;
His gospel dropped whose sweet evangel word
Repeats the song at Bethlehem Judah heard,
"From highest thrones to God be glory given,
Peace flows to earth and grace lifts man to heaven."
Aye more, for know, the Gospel always brings,
Angelic bands with blessings on their wings,

Glimpses of San Diego.

Which, scattered, cheer, like timely Summer showers;
Make deserts bloom, and even mountain towers
Rejoice and shout their glad responsive notes
To valley strains, which other upward floats.
Look then, and count! Those happy christian homes,
Where love presides and bliss of Eden comes,—
Those hallowed courts inscribed "*To Truth alone*,"
Whence prayer and praise are winged for Mercy's throne,—
Then Law's abode where power and justice meet,
And better still, yon orphans' safe retreat,—
Those honored halls whence Learning sends her gifts,—
That giant press, which, like Briareus lifts
Its hundred hands, and lo, its treasures fall
In flakes, like snow, by every cot and hall,—
Yon palace home reared up not far away,
For minds in night deprived of reason's ray,—
That mart of trade where commerce brings her spoils,—
Those whirring wheels, invention's well-laid toils,—
These curious works that tireless Art combines,
And wonders too that star-eyed Genius finds,—
Such are the gifts the glorious Gospel leaves
Wherever borne, if man its truth believes.
Like blessings now might cheer the red man's fate
Had help and hope not come, alas, so late.
For, where the Word, translated, taught and preached,
With light and life has tribe or nation reached,
Of any zone, from Arctic ice and snows
To tropics plains, where endless summer glows,

Glimpses of San Diego.

It does transform; it is the rod of strength,
That bows all wills and wins all hearts at length.
In Peter's hand, it stirred the Gentile world,
Paul bore it on where Rome her flag unfurled,
The Monk of Erfurth, found it, made it free;
All Europe shook from Black to Irish Sea,
Your Brainard held it, red-men felt its charm,
Where Cary raised it, Buddha knew alarm,
Where Martyn clasped it, dying in his youth,
The Moslem faith gives way before the truth;
Not guarded China can its power withstand,
Nor sleep unmoved the negroes' ill-starred land.
Oh, everywhere, it proves itself the rod,
That turns the nations to the Son of God.

FAILURE.

The mission fathers learned not thus the art
Of preaching Christ, whose grace renews the heart,
Nor taught that man, redeemed for worlds of bliss,
Has right divine to all he is in this.
By poor half truths, false lights amid the storm,
They stirred to fear, enslaved by chains of form,
Used hard brute force to curb the Indian will,
His freedom took. but left him Indian still.
By such misrule, his might of manhood lost—
A helmless ship, by tides and tempests tossed,
Oppressed, cast down, bewildered more and more,
He lay a wreck abandoned on the shore;

Glimpses of San Diego.

While near and far are ruins that proclaim
The mission system but a sounding name—
A failure,—this, no doubt, and something worse,
A giant evil, proved a blighting curse,

MORAL EARTHQUAKE AND RESULTS.

As when pent force breaks out in earthquake shocks,
Upturns the hills, hurls down huge mountain rocks,
Drinks rivers dry and sea-girt islands lifts,
Scoops out deep caves and joins their yawning rifts,
Turns life to death, sweeps cities out of sight,
Uncovers mines and brings their wealth to light,
So there are times when forces of the soul
Long held in check shake off and spurn control,
Take voice and shout, "attend, oh earth, our cry,
Away the Past, its trammels we defy,
We drive blind Change, our plow-share where we will,
Nor stay our course at shout of 'good' or 'ill,'
Break up repose and roll dead issues back
And leave their ruins strewe'd along our track."
Such moral earthquake, merciless and strong,
From sea to sea, from Mexico, along
The mountain crags. o'er plain and deserts drear,
Surged on its way, while men stood dumb with fear,
Loud grew the din; the halls of Congress shook;
Maine felt the jar in her remotest nook;
The sleeping prairies of the mighty West,
Awoke, amazed, and their alarm confessed.

Glimpses of San Diego.

The tremor ran to Southern everglade;
O'erleaped the streams, the grand highways of trade,
Tracked forests dense, and swept through tangled swamps,
And roused the woodmen in their quiet camps.
The nation quaked; its strongest pillars rocked;
Religion wept; philanthropy was shocked;
The wise and good had prayed for slavery's end,
But War had come arrayed as slavery's friend.
Swift rolls his car; shrill sounds his bugle blast;
The sons of Mars come gathering thick and fast;—
Shame! freedom's flag outspread above them waves,
But they must fight to make more room for slaves.
It was not so; and men may well rejoice,
God spoils their plans and brings to naught their choice;
His eye of flame their darkest scheming scans,
And with His *good*, inweaves their *evil* plans.
The shock passed by. The war-vexed land had rest.
Peace came again; when lo, at her behest,
Two empire States increased the sister band:
One wild and wide beside the Rio Grande;
One rich and vast beyond Sierras' snows,
And both to bloom with freedom's fadeless rose.

ADIEU TO THE PAST.

Adieu now the past, let its scenes drop from view,
Farewell to the old, it is time for the new;
E'en a glance at the years that fill the broad space
Between *"forty-nine,"* and that year of God's grace,

Glimpses of San Diego.

Then making its draft on the treasures of time
To bless every zone and enrich every clime,
That saw life awake and astir on the shore
Of this beautiful Bay as never before,
Would lead us too far, and delay us too long,
And lengthen too much the thin web of our song;
So, fly in your thoughts trom the "*then*" to the "*now*,"
Our Muse making haste to accomplish her vow—
Unrolling her scroll and uplifting to gaze,
Events that are sure in the near future days.

SEVEN YEARS AGO.

You query, where are we? If any don't know,
Sub rosa, I whisper, in San Diego:—
Not the same, bear in mind, that your eyes now behold,
A hopeful young damsel, not shy and not bold,
Attractive for beauty of form and of face,
Improving each day in true womanly grace,
Not faultless, we grant, yet entwining with care,
All the virtues that shine into character fair;
Not fitful, not false, nor yet vain of her wealth,
But mild like the climate and blooming with health;
Her name spreading far and her future made sure,
Her fame growing bright, not to fade but endure.
To see her as then you must brush from her brow,
All garlands of beauty adorning her now,
Her homes and her stores you must sweep out of sight,
Her churches and schools cover up as with night,

Glimpses of San Diego.

Her court house and halls from their site you must clear,
Her banks and hotels must alike disappear,
Her streets you must blot and her gardens erase,
Then chollas and brushwood for quail haunts replace,
Where rabbits, and hares, and the heron unscared,
With blackbirds and sparrows the solitude shared.
This picture preserve for its outlines are true;
And keep it in mind that your city is new,
Having gained in six years its present estate;
Through fortunes adverse and unfavoring fate;
Each year gaining strength, showing vigor unstaid—
Repressed, but not killed by her railroad delayed,
Assured that her sun is fast climbing the sky
Consuming all clouds by the flame of its eye.

MIND AND ENTERPRISE.

What city, self-risen, has history shown?
Unaided, what enterprise forward has gone?
Does not each tell of mind evolving its plan,
Into crystalized thought that must magnify man?
For proof in reply, no wide search need be made
Through dust-covered tomes and on tablets that fade,
On pillars and temples that stand and proclaim
The might that upreared them and gave them to fame;
Nor yet among ruins where riots decay
In glories despoiled, having beauty its prey.

Glimpses of San Diego.

A. E. HORTON.

Already, unsought, to my mind there has come,
A living example right here at our home.
His name, do you ask me, expecting reply?
A Yankee, you know, must the Yankee trick try,
And question the asker, which same I will do,
Hurling *point* after *point* like arrows at you.
When your section of State was almost unknown,
Who founded your city and toiled all alone?
Standing firm at his post, who wrought with a will,
Undaunted by taunts from the prophets of ill?
Who cherished the place, and with unresting care
Watched over its needs, accepting his share
Of burdens imposed—whether labor or gold,
Content to expend and the city unfold—
To claim a high rank on the ground of its worth,
And lift its fair brow to the eyes of the earth?
Who has stood at the front ever looking right on,
With *progress* his watchword till triumph is won?
Who waits for reward with a patience sublime,
Having built to his loss in advance of his time?
Hold, hold, do you cry, saying question no more,—
Write down the name HORTON with bold underscore,
Thus written uplift it to meet the world's gaze,
Entwine it with garlands of well deserved praise,
Yea, give it, in honor, high up on the page,
A place with "first things," that are richer for age.

Glimpses of San Diego.

Oh, thriving young city! thy patron, St. James,
A gospel of work and of patience proclaims;
Accept his good message; press on in thy race;
Fear not opposition; shun every disgrace;
Can fierce fires of trial thy true worth destroy?
Gold rises in value refined from alloy:
Defeat of to-day may not cloud thy to morrow,
Oft sweetest of bliss is born of deep sorrow;
So, firm as thy Loma, maintain thy design,
Undimmed, like her beacon, as faithfully shine,—
Thy light beaming clear both to guide and to bless,
Sending hope to despair, relief to distress.

" I will," in soft whisper, the city replies;
" My vow is recorded—bear witness ye skies;—
My life shall re echo the word of my saint,
1 will not by trials be stirred to complaint,
Holding worth as my aim I will cherish the pure,
Sham and shoddy refuse, choosing things that endure;
The base I will spurn, yea, all meanness despise,
Refinement approve, true excellence prize,
To learning and art give a favoring hand,
And welcome devotion to dwell in the land."

Glimpses of San Diego.

SURROUNDINGS.

Brave words thou hast spoken; they mirror thy heart,
Aglow in its courage, for acting thy part;
They prove that the summons thy waiting ears heard,
Has roused thy best nature, its energies stirred;
Has nerved thy right hand to sow marvelous change
By bay-side, on mesa, and far mountain range,
Producing such beauty as everywhere glows,
When deserts unsightly bloom fair as the rose.
Thy zeal and decision, and well expressed choice,
Inspire thy surroundings and make them rejoice;
They come with their greetings; they proffer thee aid;
Their strength is thy glory, around thee arrayed;
Thy heralds. and helpers, and subjects well known,
They give thee a kingdom and build thee a throne.

THE PACIFIC SPEAKS.

Then spake the Pacific in varying tones,
Now whisper of zephyr, now thunder's loud moans,
" Remember,fair city, my breeze-laden wings
Shall waft you the the virtue of Ponce Leon's springs;
Wild waves I will hush; my fierce tempests allay,
And show, by the calm, your appointed high-way,
Direct from your door to the hoary old East
Now hailing its day dawn, from night gloom released."

Glimpses of San Diego.

HARBOR.

The harbor came next; you might know that its speech
Would flow from its *mouth,* like the tide on the beach,
In cool, liquid words, each with meaning well-fraught,
Transparent and clear with deep currents of thought.
"You may call me your own, I am yours to command,
Give only a look or a wave of your hand,
Your ships I will shield from all danger and harm,
And fold them to rest on my Bay's brawny arm;—
Behold it, your sickle abiding its time,
To reap ripened grain from the fields of each clime."

CLIMATE.

The message of air was not uttered by word,
A breath it swept by like the gleam of a sword;
Its touch was electric and left as it passed
The city possessed of a friend tried and fast,
To whom hastening on, "I bless you," she said,
"Not only with voice, but with heart and with head.
A wing never folded ye drop me your gifts,
As night on the meadows its dew-treasure sifts,
Oh, hover above me—your welcome is sure—
Strike never more fiercely, come never less pure."

OTHERS.

Still others are waiting confidingly near,
And ask, favored city, your listening ear,

Glimpses of San Diego.

To pledge their devotion unstinted and true;
Ah, foes may be many,—your friends are not few.
The clear arching sky speaks by loveliest blue,
By beauty, the moon, rising full-orbed to view;
From far away thrones, kingly stars smile their light,
The islands, by mirage, in greeting unite;—
Do sea-nymphs provide them such marvelous dress,
And make them majestic in wild playfulness?
Yon sentinel-mountains—grand hosts of the Lord—
Stretch out their huge arms, your watch and your ward,
And often at sunrise, or daylight's decline
Enchant you with visions scarce less than divine,
Not Gobelin hues blent for royalty's eyes,
Were fairer to sight, or of brillianter dyes.

PROPHECY.

When more of thy friends pledged alike to thine aid,
Had uttered their vow, and their offerings laid
Rare gifts on thy altar—the pledge and the proof
That their to thy life is as warp to the woof,
Our Muse quite enraptured by what she had heard,
And, moved by the breathing of prophecy, stirred,
Saw thy future outspread, take form and grow clear,
Then opened her lips and thus spake as a seer:
" With horoscope lifted, I scan thy far years;
Will read thee their record, for plain it appears,
At least as it will be, if thou dost not shun
The struggle whence triumph by toil must be won.

Glimpses of San Diego.

Thy rank is assured and it will be confessed,
Detraction will cease—thy wrongs be redressed,
The shadows around thee shall vanish like mist,
Thy growth, predetermined, no arm can resist;
The Jericho walls that have girt thee about
Shall acknowledge thy faith and fall at thy shout,
Shall yield thee their riches confessing thy might
But voices the claim of thy sure vested right.
A highway of nations must pass at thy door;
All lands must in tribute spread wider thy power,
And, taught by thy word, cheered and blessed by thy light,
Shall break from their bondage and flee from their night."

OUR NATION.

God sifted the nations; and then to complete
His far-reaching plan of grain from clean wheat,
He chose virgin soil, brought appliances rare,
Turned over the fallow and sowed it with care,
Then patiently waited till germs should appear,
As patiently waited for corn in the ear.
How precious that harvest words fail me to tell!
Its reapers in song sounded tyranny's knell,
Their pæon of freedom waked echoing tones
That shook to their downfall earth's crime-guarded thrones.
Behold our Republic! Its banner unfurled,
Sent strength to the weak all over the world.
Hark! The century shout. It is harvest again!
Ho, reapers afield! forty millions of men!

Glimpses of San Diego.

RESPONSIVE ECHOES.

Plymouth Rock is afar, so too Bunker Hill,
But their image is *here.* Their memories thrill
Every chord of our souls. Bright names ye are *ours,*
And ages to come shall entwine you with flowers.
Ho, Warren and Ledyard! Montgomery too!
Ho, Kalb and Pulaski! the warder means you!
The flag that ye died for in glory still waves;
Beside the Pacific are tears for your graves.

CONCLUSION.

O city of nations! "good morn to thy fame,"
May error not cloud the bright sky of thy name!
New England will give thee her zeal for the right,
The West will contribute her ardor and might,
The South will bequeath thee the grace of her ways;
Up! prove a world's blessing! On! win a world's praise!
Spread out to all nations thy peace-laden wings,
And fail not to honor the KING OF THE KINGS.